Abenaki,
The Indian Pony

A little horse's adventure
across the country

written & illustrated

by Denise F. Brown

Abenaki, the Indian Pony
A little horse's adventure across the country
ISBN-10:
0985263946
ISBN-13:
978-0-9852639-4-2

Credits

Special thanks to
Emily Brown
Loretta Brown
Laura Askham Brown
and John O'Sullivan
for their help and participation in writing this children's story.

Concept, illustrated, and published by Denise F. Brown
www.raccoonstudios.com
Portsmouth, New Hampshire

www.raccoonstudios.com
Raccoon Studios, 692 Sagamore Avenue, Portsmouth, NH 03801 USA 603-436-0788

One morning the sun rose in the East. It was a golden sunrise filled with oranges and pinks that melted against the Atlantic Ocean's beaches. The sun was so bright that it woke Abenaki, a young Indian pony who lived along the coast of northeastern America.

He was very hungry so he went for a walk to search for his favorite food. He knew exactly where to find it.

Abenaki trotted to a nearby river called the Piscataqua. Along the banks of the river, he found a patch of tender green rye grass and sweet strawberries to eat. Then he tipped his head down to have a drink of water where fresh water flowed into the river. A splashy little fish was swimming by the shore.

Abenaki asked the fish, "What are you doing?" The fish said, "I am waiting for delicious bugs to eat." "I see", said Abenaki, as he ate more grass and strawberries.

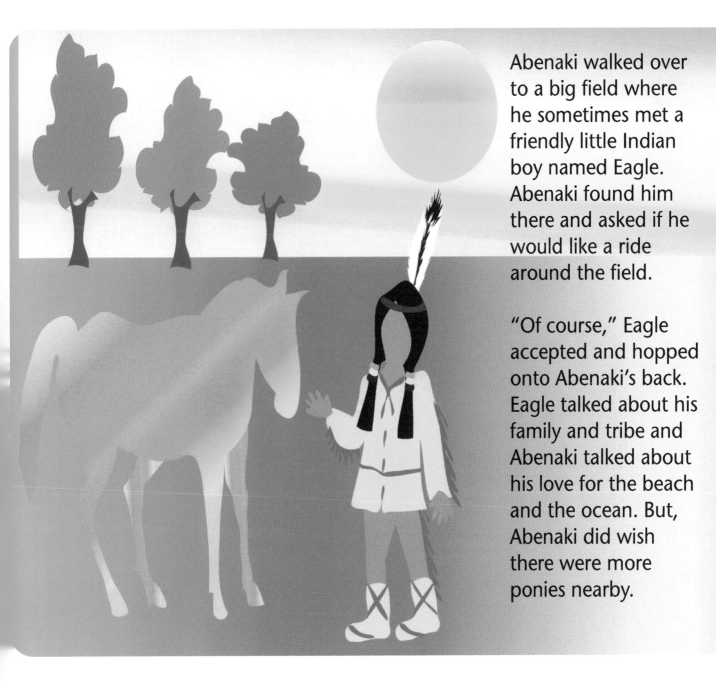

Abenaki walked over to a big field where he sometimes met a friendly little Indian boy named Eagle. Abenaki found him there and asked if he would like a ride around the field.

"Of course," Eagle accepted and hopped onto Abenaki's back. Eagle talked about his family and tribe and Abenaki talked about his love for the beach and the ocean. But, Abenaki did wish there were more ponies nearby.

5

Then Eagle said, "I have heard of another Great Ocean in the West. Maybe there are more ponies there. Let's go and find this ocean!"

Abenaki agreed, "We will follow the sun to the west!"

A noisy bluebird wished them luck.

As they walked along a winding path, suddenly a rabbit jumped out in front of them. A hungry fox was chasing him! The fox took one look at Abenaki and Eagle, and ran away as fast as he could.

"Thank you for saving my life!" said the rabbit. "Where are you going?" "We are going out west to find another Great Ocean," said Abenaki. They took the rabbit to his family's den and went on their way.

Abenaki and Eagle rode on and passed through the White Mountains. There they saw an outcrop of large rocks and boulders high on a cliff. The rocks looked like the face of an old man.

An eagle flew over them and cast a big shadow on the rocks. He waved his great wings as if to say good morning, I will protect both of you.

They grew tired and decided to rest in a cool cave that they found, where an Indian tribe had once lived.

There were many drawings on the walls of the cave. One was of a pony and a rider leading a long line of ponies.

9

After their rest, they left the cave and walked for many days until they reached the Great Lakes.

They went swimming in a small pond nearby and saw a brown moose drinking water from the pond's edge.

A beautiful dragonfly and a sleepy turtle were sunning themselves on the shore.

The ground stretched out into a vast prairie for many miles. Deer and antelope and a white buffalo were grazing for grass.

A friendly cowbird swooped down and landed on Abenaki's back for a moment, to catch a horsefly.

Abenaki was so thrilled that he galloped ahead with Eagle holding on tightly to his mane. He never felt so free.

11

Later, they took a short rest in a tall forest. As they traveled further, they found a huge canyon. They wondered how far they had come?

A great thunderbird flew over them and cast his shadow in front of them. This was a sign that their journey would be safe.

When they reached a steep mountain range capped with snow, they knew they must climb over it to continue west.

The mountains were rocky but the climbing was exciting and the views were spectacular.

They saw many hungry bears hunting for food.

The mountains ended at a hot, sandy desert, where a spotted gecko and a noisy rattlesnake appeared in the shadow of a cactus. Abenaki and Eagle almost didn't see them there.

The gecko asked, "Where are you going?"

Abenaki answered, "We've been traveling across the country to find another Great Ocean. We're almost at the end of our journey and hope to meet other ponies who are just as adventurous as we are."

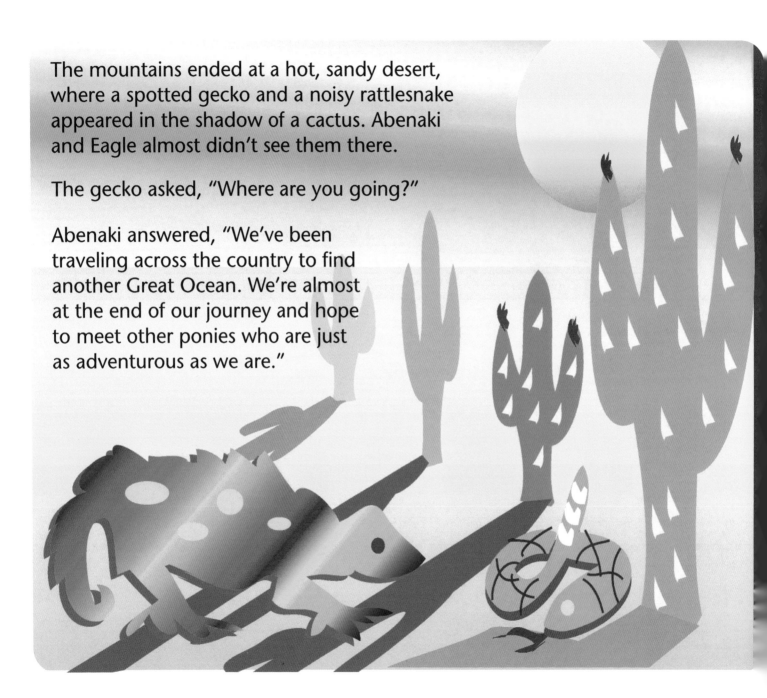

The gecko wished them well, so they continued on toward the tall redwood trees on the west coast.

Abenaki and Eagle admired the trees, for they were the tallest that they had ever seen.

An quiet owl flew around them and waved them on as they left the dark forest.

15

One day, it was late in the afternoon and the big orange sun was setting into the water. After traveling for many days, Abenaki and Eagle finally reached the Great Ocean on the west coast!

It is called the Pacific Ocean and what Abenaki and the little Indian boy saw there made them so happy...

...There were many other ponies on the beach watching the brilliant sunset!

The ponies exchanged stories and talked about exciting friends and animals they met all across America.

A few of the ponies mentioned they had seen groups of ponies and Indian tribes gathered in a place called Scottsdale, Arizona. They had seen many tepees set up in the open fields.

"What a great place for the ponies to have a reunion with the Indian tribes!" remarked Abenaki.

So they all agreed and decided to make a trail together to the southwest.

The ponies asked Abenaki and Eagle to lead the trail.

The ponies walked until the day turned into night. They saw a falling star over the mountains.

It was too dark to continue, so they decided to sleep under the starry sky.

When they awoke in the morning, they saw many colorful tepees.

There were Indian girls and boys all around, preparing fresh food to eat. They placed buckets of water on the ground for the ponies to drink.

The Indians held a big party for them at the end of their long trail. The ponies talked about where they lived across the country.

The "Trail of Painted Ponies" became a great event. Abenaki was truly happy.

All the ponies and the Indian boy, Eagle, would remember this trip for as long as they lived.

The ponies and children enjoyed visiting with their new friends and took a long rest before they traveled back to their homes across the country.

Abenaki and Eagle waved goodbye as they began their journey home to the northeast.

They couldn't wait to
tell everyone of their
great adventure
across the country.

It was time to go home!

—The End—

About the author / illustrator

The author and illustrator, Denise F. Brown of Portsmouth, New Hampshire, is a graphic designer, illustrator, photographer and watercolor/acrylic painter.

Brown, along with husband, John O'Sullivan, owns Ad-Cetera Graphics and Raccoon Studios of Portsmouth. She is the author/illustrator of "*Wind, Wild Horse Rescue*" an adventure book about mustangs and illustrator of "Tugboat River Rescue" a true story about a tugboat rescue.

She is well known for her stunning watercolors of Seacoast scenes, architectural renderings, horse illustrations, and her pony figurine designs with The Trail of Painted Ponies. She is also the creator of the popular series of children's coloring books, "*Ted Gets Out*", which celebrates the adventures of one of her cats.

See Denise's work at:

www.windwildhorse.com
www.tugboatrescue.com
www.raccoonstudios.com
www.deervisitsNubble

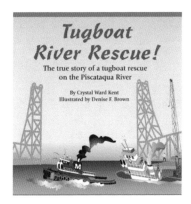

"Tugboat River Rescue"
children's book
written by Crystal Ward Kent
illustrated by Denise F. Brown
www.tugboatrescue.com

"Wind, Wild Horse Rescue"
about the plight of mustangs today
written and illustrated by
Denise F. Brown
www.windwildhorse.com
ages 9 to adult

"A Deer Visits Nubble Lighthouse"
children's book
written and illustrated
by Denise F. Brown
edited by Crystal Ward Kent
www.deervisitsNubble.com
www.raccoonstudios.com

"Ted the Cat"
Children's Coloring Books
illustrated by
Denise F. Brown
edited by
John F. O'Sullivan
www.raccoonstudios.com

This book was inspired by

"Abenaki,
The Indian Pony Life Story"

An original hand painted pony sculpture
by Denise F. Brown,
one of twenty finalists in the 2006
"The Trail of Painted Ponies"
National Art Competition

Special credit of thanks to the

"The Trail of Painted Ponies"

for encouraging artists in their endeavors
and for their philanthropic efforts
involving many great non-profit causes
including to help wild horses.

Made in the USA
Charleston, SC
01 April 2013

Abenaki, The Indian Pony

A little horse's adventure across the country

written & illustrated by Denise F. Brown

Abenaki is a wild pony from the East coast. One day he decides to go for a walking adventure across the country and meets many friends along the way. This beautifully illustrated story is about animals and different locations he sees from the Atlantic to the Pacific.

Denise and Abenaki,
"The Indian Pony Life Story"
An original hand painted pony sculpture
by Denise F. Brown
for The Trail of Painted Ponies competition

© 2013 Denise F. Brown
www.raccoonstudios.com

ISBN-10:
0985263946
ISBN-13:
978-0-9852639-4-2

$14.99

ISBN 978-0-9852639-4-2
51499>

9 780985 263942